EDGE
BOOKS

ZOMBIES

THE TRUTH BEHIND
History's Terrifying Flesh-Eaters

by Steve Goldsworthy

Raintree is an imprint of Capstone Global Library Limited, a company incorporated in England and Wales having its registered office at 7 Pilgrim Street, London, EC4V 6LB – Registered company number: 6695582

www.raintree.co.uk
myorders@raintree.co.uk

Edited by Aaron Sautter
Designed by Bobbie Nuytten
Picture research by Gina Kammer
Production by Laura Manthe
Printed in China

ISBN 978 1 4747 0448 9
19 18 17 16 15
10 9 8 7 6 5 4 3 2 1

British Library Cataloguing in Publication Data
A full catalogue record for this book is available from the British Library.

Acknowledgements
Alamy: © AF archive, 24, 29, © Mary Evans Picture Library, 23, © Moviestore collection Ltd, 26; Bridgeman Images: By permission of the Governors of Stonyhurst College/Ms 59 fol.50r Mass for Burial of the Dead, from the Hours of Madeleine Levesque, c.1480 (gouache & bodycolour on vellum), Maitre Francois (15th century), 21; Corbis: © Bettmann, cover, © Bettmann, 1, NurPhoto/© Impact Press Group, 20; Getty Images: Duncan Walker, 15, 27, G. DAGLI ORTI/DEA, 6, Werner Forman, 8; iStockphoto: Renphoto, 5; Jeff L. Davis, 17; Landov: HotSpot, 16; Mary Evans Picture Library, 18; Shutterstock: Alex Malikov, (top) 10, breaker213, 4, Elenarts, 13, Gennady Dolgov, 19, Pixel 4 Images, cover, 1, sittitap, 14, trappy76, 7, Ttatty, 9, Valentyn Hontovyy, (bottom) 10, Webspark, 25, WELBURNSTUART, 28, Yuri Megel, 22; Wikimedia: Antoine Wiertz, 11, Cathedral Library, Esztergom, 12

Design Elements
Shutterstock: Ensuper (grunge background), Larysa Ray (grunge frames), Slava Gerj (grunge scratched background)

We would like to thank David Gilmore, Professor of Anthropology at Stony Brook University, New York, for his invaluable help in the preparation of this book.

CONTENTS

THE WORLD OF ZOMBIES

They stagger towards you. Their outstretched arms are covered in rotting flesh. Fresh from the grave, they seem unstoppable in their advance. While moaning and grinding their teeth, they want only one thing – to eat you! You've just stumbled into the nightmare world of zombies.

There are many types of zombies in scary stories, but they all have a few things in common. Zombies are the bodies of people who have died and then risen from the grave. These monsters aren't alive, but are considered to be **undead**. Zombies also have no will or mind of their own. They act under the power of something or someone else. Sometimes it is a magical spell cast by a **voodoo** priest. But more often it is the intense desire to eat warm, human flesh.

From today's films and TV series to comic books and video games, zombies seem to be everywhere. But long ago people often thought these terrifying monsters were real. Tales of these stumbling, flesh-eating **corpses** have haunted people for thousands of years.

undead no longer alive but still able to move and take action

voodoo religion that began in Africa; voodoo involves the worship of ancestral spirits and the use of magic

corpse dead body

FACT: The word "zombie" was first used by historian Robert Southey in his book *History of Brazil*. The book was published in 1810.

CHAPTER 1
ZOMBIES IN THE ANCIENT WORLD

Ancient zombie myths can be found all over the world. Most ancient **cultures** had legends of the dead coming back to life. Stories of the walking dead were often meant to scare people into good behaviour. In many ancient stories, gods or evil spirits sent the living dead to attack the living or to teach them a lesson.

Ancient cultures from Europe, Africa and the Middle East all had a long history of zombie stories. One of the earliest written stories to mention the living dead was the *Epic of Gilgamesh*. This 4,000-year-old story from Mesopotamia describes how the goddess Ishtar became angry with humans. As a punishment she threatened to raise the dead to eat the living.

Ishtar was worshipped as the goddess of love and war in Mesopotamia.

EVIDENCE IN THE GROUND

Evidence that people believed in zombies isn't found only in ancient stories and legends. **Archaeologists** have found physical evidence that suggests some ancient people may have believed in zombies. At one 10,000-year-old site in Syria, many bodies were discovered with their skulls destroyed. Others had no head at all. Some experts believe ancient people did this to prevent the dead from rising to attack the living.

culture people's way of life, ideas, customs and traditions

archaeologist scientist who studies how people lived in the past

ANCIENT MYTHS AND LEGENDS

Legends from ancient Egypt show how people believed the dead could return to life. In one such myth, Egypt's first ruler, Osiris, was murdered. His wife Isis then used magic to bring him back to life. Osiris later became an Egyptian god and the ruler of the **afterlife**.

The Egyptians believed that, like Osiris, the spirits of the dead could travel to a new world after death. But to achieve this, the dead needed their bodies to make the journey. To provide the dead with what they needed, the Egyptians preserved the bodies of the dead by **mummifying** them. The dead were then buried along with their belongings and supplies needed for the afterlife. The Egyptians believed the dead then rose again in their mummified bodies to live forever in the afterlife.

According to legend, the god Osiris was killed by his brother Set. After Osiris was brought back to life, he became the Lord of the Dead.

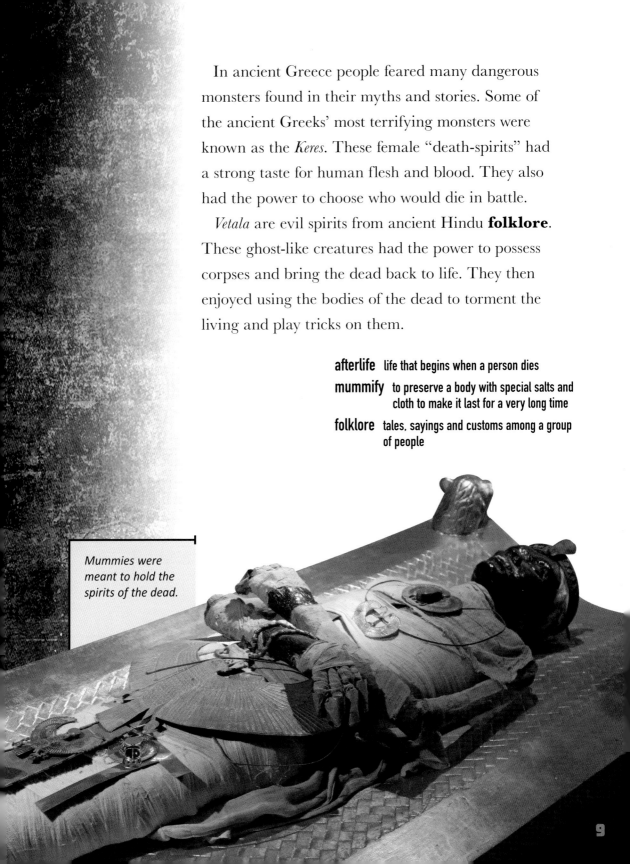

In ancient Greece people feared many dangerous monsters found in their myths and stories. Some of the ancient Greeks' most terrifying monsters were known as the *Keres*. These female "death-spirits" had a strong taste for human flesh and blood. They also had the power to choose who would die in battle.

Vetala are evil spirits from ancient Hindu **folklore**. These ghost-like creatures had the power to possess corpses and bring the dead back to life. They then enjoyed using the bodies of the dead to torment the living and play tricks on them.

afterlife life that begins when a person dies

mummify to preserve a body with special salts and cloth to make it last for a very long time

folklore tales, sayings and customs among a group of people

Mummies were meant to hold the spirits of the dead.

CHAPTER 2
MEDIEVAL ZOMBIE FOLKLORE

For people in the Middle Ages (c. AD 500 to 1450), graveyards were places to fear at night. Many people believed the dead did not always stay in their graves. Wandering through a cemetery in the dark could bring you face to face with an angry walking corpse. In these people's minds, zombies were very real. They felt that as long as there was flesh on a body, it could become one of the walking dead.

MISTAKEN FOR DEAD

Today doctors know how to treat many diseases and illnesses. But during **medieval** times, most people didn't know much about medicine or disease. Sometimes this led to sick people being mistaken for zombies. When people were very sick they could fall into a **coma**. Their breathing and heart rate would become extremely slow, and they could appear to be dead. These poor people could be buried, only to wake up inside a grave.

As others walked by the graveyard, they might hear the cries of those who had been buried alive. Sometimes the victims would be dug up again. But when people lifted the lid of the coffin, they'd be greeted by a horrible sight. The victims had most likely **suffocated** inside the coffin, and their clothes might be torn to shreds. Their hands, legs and head might be bloodied from trying to escape. The body probably looked like a member of the living dead.

medieval having to do with the period of history between AD 500 and 1450

coma state of deep unconsciousness from which it is very hard to wake up

suffocate to die from lack of oxygen

In the Middle Ages people with serious illnesses were sometimes mistakenly buried alive.

RISE OF THE DEAD

When medieval people saw bloodied bodies in freshly dug graves they often became very frightened. This fear, along with people's religious beliefs, helped to create many myths about how the dead might return to life.

People with strong religious beliefs thought the dead had to be given proper burials. If the dead weren't buried correctly, it was thought they could return to life. Dying suddenly or being killed violently could also trigger the dead to return to life.

Another popular idea was that evil spirits could bring the dead back to life. These spirits would enter the bodies of the dead and then rise from the grave. It was believed that a physical body gave these wicked spirits the ability to roam about in the world of the living.

Many medieval artists created artwork in the style of Danse Macabre, or the "Dance of Death". These images usually show the dead leading the living to their graves.

MEDIEVAL EYEWITNESS REPORTS

Many medieval people believed that especially wicked people could return from death to torment the living. In 1196 William Newburgh wrote several stories about reported zombie cases. One story describes a woman who was terrified by visits from her dead husband. He had badly mistreated her while he was alive. He supposedly continued to torment her as an undead monster.

Soon, several men decided to help. They reportedly chased the dead man through the forest one night, but couldn't catch him. The next day they decided to dig up his corpse. The men said that the body had fresh mud on its legs from the night before!

FACT: In Iceland, dying at sea was considered to be a horrible death. People thought dying in this way could result in the dead rising again.

ACTIONS OF THE UNDEAD

Today's zombies usually just wander around looking for their next meal. But unlike modern zombies, in medieval tales the undead were often intelligent. They usually had a purpose for their actions. Their intelligence was what scared people the most. They were often angry and had a plan to get their revenge on the living. These solitary monsters would wait in the shadows to attack their victims. In other stories these creatures also fiercely guarded their buried treasure from thieves.

FACT: During medieval times the undead were usually known as revenants. The term comes from the Latin word *reveniens*, which means "returning". Stories about undead revenants came from all parts of Western Europe including Iceland, England, France and Germany.

Zombies in medieval tales often actively hunted for their living enemies to torment them or to seek revenge for their own murders.

ZOMBIES AROUND THE WORLD

Tales during the Middle Ages described zombies with a variety of physical features and characteristics. In Scandinavia some people feared a zombie called a *draugr*. Rotting and foul-smelling, evil *draugrs* were described as being as "black as death". But in some tales, these zombies could also be very pale or even blue. Sometimes they swelled in size after death and possessed great strength.

In Scandinavian myths evil draugrs often appear as rotting corpses. These creatures rose from the dead to guard treasures or torment those who wronged them in life.

Stories from China feature undead monsters called *jiang shi*. These zombies were said to be created when a person's soul failed to leave the body. This could be caused by an unnatural death, or if a person was a terrible troublemaker in life. *Jiang shi* had very stiff arms and legs and couldn't bend them. They could only move around by hopping. Like other zombies *jiang shi* were often covered in rotting flesh.

Jiang shi *were described as being green-white in colour and covered in mould. They also had long, sharp nails on their hands.*

FACT: In Arabia, zombies were known as ghouls. These horrifying creatures often ate human flesh, whether a person was alive or dead. Sometimes ghouls even took the form of the person they had just eaten.

CHAPTER 3
HUNTING THE LIVING DEAD

The threat of undead monsters rising from the grave was very real for many medieval people. But they also believed that zombies had certain weaknesses. They were ready to defend themselves against the monsters. Some people used special religious **rituals** against the undead. Others performed strange burial practices. And some people even believed that they knew how to kill zombies for good.

ritual ceremony involving a set of religious actions

Christian burials in the Middle Ages involved reciting several prayers for the dead, blessing gravesides, and sprinkling bodies and coffins with holy water.

PROPER BURIALS

In the Middle Ages people believed the best defence against zombies was to keep the dead from rising in the first place. This began with the careful burial of bodies. People in most of Europe believed that the dead needed proper Christian burials to be at rest. This involved reciting certain prayers and placing the body so that its feet faced east.

Some people also used "corpse doors" to remove dead bodies from homes. When someone died, the body would be carried out feet-first through the door. Carrying bodies to the grave this way supposedly prevented the dead from seeing where they were going. This in turn kept the dead from returning the same way they had come.

After removing dead bodies, people often bricked up "corpse doors" to keep the dead from returning to their homes.

EXTREME MEASURES

Sometimes people feared that normal burials weren't enough to prevent the dead from rising. In these cases people used extreme methods to keep a body in the ground. One method involved pinning the body to the ground. People drove spikes through a dead body and into the earth. In Scandinavia they first tied a dead body's toes together. Then they inserted needles into the body's feet to keep it from walking out of its grave.

In many cases, people believed that bodies had to be tied up and buried quickly. These bodies were often sewn up in cloth shrouds. Sometimes they were also tied up with rope before being placed into a coffin. The coffin was then nailed shut and buried deep in the ground.

Skeletons in Bulgaria have been found pinned to the ground with iron rods through their chests. The rods supposedly helped to make sure that the dead stayed in their graves.

Sometimes bodies were buried in pieces to keep them from returning to life. People even buried body parts in separate places to make sure the dead could not crawl out of their graves. Still another way to prevent the dead from rising was to dump bodies in a river. Many people believed that water was a natural barrier between the worlds of the living and the dead.

FACT: In Ireland, skeletons from the 700s have been found with stones in their mouths. At that time, many people believed the mouth was the doorway to the body. A stone in a body's mouth was thought to keep the soul from re-entering the body and returning it to life.

DESTROYING THE UNDEAD

Medieval folklore describes several ways that people could destroy flesh-eating zombies. But how do you kill something that's already dead?

To destroy a zombie, it helped to know the monster's weaknesses. Zombies in many stories could roam around only at night. The living dead had to return to their graves by sunrise. During the day people could dig up the dead creature and bury it again using a religious ritual. To do this, a priest or religious leader first sprinkled the body with holy water. Then he would recite certain prayers to **redeem** the zombie's soul. This process was thought to allow the dead to finally be at rest in the grave.

The destruction of the brain was also a well-known way to kill zombies. Monster hunters would wait until a zombie returned to its grave. Then after digging up the corpse, they'd destroy the head or remove it completely.

redeem to free from the consequences of sinful behaviour

war hammer

mace

Some medieval people believed that digging up a zombie and burning it to ashes would destroy the monster for good.

FACT: In Arabian tales, ghouls could be destroyed with one blow from a sword. But a second strike would just bring them back to life again!

CHAPTER 4

ZOMBIES EVERYWHERE

Today zombies seem to be everywhere. They can be found in films, TV series, books, comics, video games and more. But the monsters in today's stories are very different from those in stories of long ago. Modern zombies are created differently, behave differently and can be destroyed in many different ways.

MAKING MODERN ZOMBIES

In modern stories, zombies can be created in several ways. In 1932 the first modern zombie film, *White Zombie*, featured zombies created by an evil magician. He used black magic to control people's minds and turn them into zombified slaves.

In modern zombie films the monsters often attack people in large packs.

ZOMBIE OUTBREAK

The idea of zombies as **reanimated** corpses was later made popular through films directed by George A Romero. In his films the bodies of the dead are brought back to life by strange **radiation** from space.

Another popular idea is that zombies are created through the spread of a zombie disease. If a zombie bites someone, that person will quickly become ill and die. The victim later rises from the dead as a new zombie. In these stories there is little hope for humans. The more people zombies bite, the faster the disease spreads. The outbreak spreads like wildfire until every person is either eaten or turned into a zombie.

reanimate   to restore to life or consciousness
radiation   tiny particles sent out from
              radioactive materials

MODERN ZOMBIE BEHAVIOUR

In most modern stories, zombies behave very differently from those in medieval tales. They shuffle along aimlessly until they smell a human or hear a noise. They only attack if they see a possible meal of warm flesh. Some modern zombies like eating human brains. But most of them crave any warm flesh they can get. These monsters are often easy to kill because they move so slowly and don't defend themselves.

Some modern zombies are terrifying, rampaging monsters. These creatures are usually fast runners that never get tired and never stop. They often attack by swarming over victims in large groups.

Zombies in most modern stories are slow-moving, mindless creatures. They're usually easy to kill or outrun.

VOODOO ZOMBIES

Several modern ideas about zombies come from old voodoo traditions and folklore from Haiti. In the late 1800s and early 1900s, people in Haiti often believed that sorcerers called *bokors* could turn living people into zombies. *Bokors* were thought to first give victims powerful drugs to make them appear dead. They would then revive the people in secret and make them into slaves. The *bokors* were said to keep their victims drugged in order to control them. They didn't want their zombie slaves to think for themselves or disobey commands. These people usually moved slowly and rarely talked, making them seem like brain-dead zombies. Some people in Haiti still believe that *bokors* are creating such voodoo zombies today.

MODERN ZOMBIE DEFENCES

In today's zombie stories people are usually prepared to battle against the flesh-eating monsters. They'll use any weapon available to kill the walking dead, including guns, shovels, swords, axes and bats. The target is always the zombie's head. To kill these creatures for good, their brains must be completely destroyed.

SCARY THRILLS

People have feared the living dead for thousands of years. But today that fear has turned into a thrill for many people. Horror fans love the chills provided by flesh-eating zombies. From films to video games, zombies are more popular today than ever. As long as people enjoy being scared, new tales about these undead monsters will be told for years to come.

ZOMBIES IN POPULAR CULTURE

TITLE (YEAR)	MEDIA	ZOMBIE TYPE
White Zombie (1932)	film	mind-controlled
I Am Legend (1954)	novel	slow movers
Michael Jackson: Thriller (1983)	short film	slow movers
Plants vs Zombies (2009)	video game	slow movers
Pirates of the Caribbean: On Stranger Tides (2011)	film	mind-controlled
Minecraft (2011)	video game	slow movers
Munchkin Zombies (2011)	card game	slow movers
ParaNorman (2012)	film	slow movers
Warm Bodies (2013)	film	slow movers/fast rampagers

Modern zombie films and TV series feature some of the scariest monsters ever seen on screen.

GLOSSARY

afterlife life that begins when a person dies

archaeologist scientist who studies how people lived in the past

coma state of deep unconsciousness from which it is very hard to wake up

corpse dead body

culture people's way of life, ideas, customs and traditions

folklore tales, sayings and customs among a group of people

medieval having to do with the period of history between AD 500 and 1450

mummify to preserve a body with special salts and cloth to make it last for a very long time

radiation tiny particles sent out from radioactive material

reanimate to restore to life or consciousness

redeem to free from the consequences of sinful behaviour

revenant body or spirit of someone who has returned from the dead

ritual ceremony involving a set of religious actions

suffocate to die from lack of oxygen

undead no longer alive but still able to move and take action

voodoo religion that began in Africa; voodoo involves the worship of ancestral spirits and the use of magic

BOOKS

The Undead (The Twilight Realm), Jim Pipe (Wayland, 2011)

Zombies: Everything Vital about these Undead Monsters (Girl's Guide to Everything Unexplained), Jen Jones (Raintree, 2012)

Zombies vs Mummies: Clash of the Living Dead (Monster Wars), Michael O'Hearn (Raintree, 2012)

WEBSITES

www.news.discovery.com/history/history-zombies-12-6-4.htm
Learn about the history of supposed voodoo zombies in Haiti and some of the science behind people's beliefs about them.

www.tor.com/blogs/2010/09/historical-zombies-mummies-the-odyssey-and-beyond
Learn about beliefs people had about the living dead from ancient Egypt through the Middle Ages.

www.wordsicle.com/zombie-timeline/
Read all about the history of zombies in popular culture from ancient myths and legends to modern Hollywood films.

INDEX